TOP HAT
*Stack no. 4 –
Railway Tug*
Only Star Tug with a
raised wheelhouse.

D0590721

WARRIOR
*Stack no. 5 –
Harbour Tug*
Very strong, but
sometimes clumsy.
Will tackle any job.

HERCULES
*Stack no. 6 – Ocean-
going Tug*
One of the leaders of
the fleet. Very proud
and rather aloof.

SUNSHINE
*Stack no. 7 –
Harbour Switcher*
Newest member of
the Star Fleet. Works
mainly with Ten
Cents.

TITLES AVAILABLE IN BUZZ BOOKS

First published 1990 by Buzz Books,
an imprint of the Octopus Publishing Group,
Michelin House, 81 Fulham Road, London, SW3 6RB.

LONDON MELBOURNE AUCKLAND

Text © 1990 William Heinemann Ltd

Illustrations © 1990 William Heinemann Ltd
Story by Fiona Hardwick
Illustrations by The County Studio
Based on the television series TUGS produced by TUGS Ltd
for Clearwater Features (1986) Ltd and TVS Television,
© TUGS 1988.

ISBN 1 85591 012 8

Printed and bound in the UK by BPCC Paulton Books Ltd.

• A TUGS ADVENTURE •

KIDNAPPED!

Story by Fiona Hardwick
Illustrations by The County Studio

It was Sunshine's first season as part of the
Star Fleet, and he loved being part of the
harbour team. He worked hard, doing his
best to help Ten Cents and the other tugs.

When there were spare moments between
jobs, he listened to the others swap tales of
their past adventures.

"The old paddle steamers were so
elegant," said O.J.

"That's nothing compared to the luxury
liners these days, m'dears," Hercules joined
in. "I remember the day the Duchess was
launched – my word, what an honour it
was to be part of her flotilla!"

Top Hat came over.

"What's happening, chaps?" he asked.

"O.J. and Hercules were telling me about paddle steamers and liners," said Sunshine. "They've had loads of exciting adventures!"

"Haven't we all, dear boy, haven't we all," interrupted Top Hat grandly. "My, I could tell you some stories!"

"Oh, yes please." Sunshine was waiting.

"Ah well, um, I can't seem to recall anything in particular now – another time perhaps. Haven't we got a lot of work to do?" said Top Hat, changing the subject.

O.J. grinned. "You're right there, Top Hat. That's enough tales for today, Sunshine – let's get on."

The tugs went off in different directions, carrying out the orders Captain Star had given them earlier. Warrior was shifting a cargo of wood, so Sunshine took charge of Lord Stinker, the rubbish barge. It wasn't a very nice job, but someone had to do it.

10

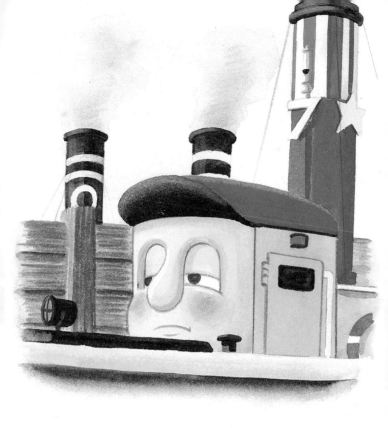

Normally, Sunshine didn't mind doing his share of the nasty jobs, but today, after listening to the others, he was discontented.

"If only I could have an adventure," he sighed. "There's nothing very exciting about collecting the rubbish."

Sunshine didn't notice that two Z Stacks behind the wall had overheard him.

"So little Sunshine's bored is he? What a pity!" whispered one of them.

"Let's give him an adventure he won't forget in a hurry!"

The two stacks bobbed up and down as the tugs rocked with wicked laughter.

Sunshine had just finished the rubbish,
when suddenly he felt two tugs shove into
the back of him.

"Hey watch it fellas! What the . . . Help!"

"Quiet," said one of the tugs in a
menacing voice, "or we'll use this
dynamite. There's enough here to blow a
miserable little tug like you sky high!"

Sunshine was brave, but not that brave. He decided to co-operate.

The tugs gave Sunshine instructions where to go, keeping behind him all the time. They travelled through parts of the harbour that Sunshine had never seen. Now it was dark, and Sunshine was lost.

"OK, turn left here," said one of the tugs.

Sunshine saw he was in a dark and dingy shed that looked as if it hadn't been used for years. It was cold and dirty. Sunshine felt rather small and a little bit scared.

The kidnappers tied him up.

"Why have you brought me here?" he asked, trying to see the kidnappers.

"We . . . er, we . . . er have a devious plan!" said one of the kidnappers, doing his best to sound convincing.

"Right, we have work to do – don't get lonely, will you?" sniggered the other.

The tugs left Sunshine alone in the shed.

16

Sunshine looked thoughtful.

"I must try to escape."

He was securely moored to an old jetty.

"What can I use to free myself?" he said.

He noticed a piece of rusty metal sticking out of the water.

"It's worth a try," he said, manoeuvring himself next to it.

17

In the harbour, Ten Cents was worried.

"Sunshine should have been back from doing the rubbish ages ago. Have you seen him, O.J.?"

"No. Perhaps he's in trouble. I'll organise a search party."

"Good idea, O.J. Come on Star Tugs! We've got to find Sunshine!"

18

Zorran steamed by.

"Problems, boys?" he said, gloatingly.
"You should keep that overgrown bath toy
under control."

"Shut up Zorran, and give us some help."

For once, Zorran agreed and teamed up
with Big Mac.

"No funny business, OK Zorran?"

Ten Cents and O.J. retraced Sunshine's route to the Municipal Waste Co. to look for clues, but it was no good. Sunshine had completely disappeared.

"It's hopeless," sighed Ten Cents. "We'll have to go back and tell the Captain."

The tugs went slowly back to Star Pier.

Ten Cents was just wondering what he could tell Captain Star, when he heard a loud tooting.

"That's Sunshine!" exclaimed Ten Cents. "Where have you been all this time?"

Sunshine was red-faced with all the
excitement.

"Listen, listen. I have just had an
incredible adventure. I was kidnapped!"

"What? Preposterous idea!" Top Hat
sniffed loudly.

"It's true! Two enormous tugs crept up
and kidnapped me. I fought iike mad, but
they threatened to blow me up with
dynamite. They forced me to go to the far
side of the harbour, and tied me up in a
creepy dark shed."

23

"So why are you here now?" asked
Warrior, confused.

"Because I escaped! Those kidnappers
didn't frighten me. As soon as they were
busy, I cut myself free."

By now, Zip and Zug were in the
harbour. When they spotted Sunshine, they
were very surprised. As Sunshine continued
his story, they started looking guilty, but
no-one noticed – except Zorran.

24

"So you got your adventure after all, Sunshine," said O.J. with a big smile.

"Yes, but who did it?" asked Ten Cents. "And why should anyone want to kidnap Sunshine?"

Suddenly everyone had turned round and was looking at Zorran.

"Now come on you lot! Of course it
wasn't me – I even helped to look for the
little troublemaker, didn't I?"

"He's safe now, that's all that matters,"
said O.J.

"And I can't wait to tell that gossip,
Scuttle Butt Pete!"

With a cheeky grin and a whistle, Sunshine set off for his mooring.

Zip and Zug tried to sneak away before there were any more difficult questions.

Too late. Looking even nastier than usual, Zorran stopped them and said:

"You bungling idiots! See what happens when you try to do things on your own! I'm in charge round here – so listen. Double dredger work for both of you, now!"

"It's all your fault." "It was your idea!" "No, it wasn't!" "Yes, it was!"

Zip and Zug argued bitterly all the way across to the dredger.

ZORRAN

THE Z STACKS

ZORRAN
Stack no. 1 –
Harbour Tug
Leader of the Z
Stacks. A mean,
tough character.

ZEBEDEE
Stack no. 2 –
Harbour Tug

ZAK
Stack no. 3 –
Harbour Tug